Dear Parent:
Your child's love of reading starts here!

Every child learns to read in a different way and at his or her own speed. Some go back and forth between reading levels and read favorite books again and again. Others read through each level in order. You can help your young reader improve and become more confident by encouraging his or her own interests and abilities. From books your child reads with you to the first books he or she reads alone, there are I Can Read Books for every stage of reading:

SHARED READING
Basic language, word repetition, and whimsical illustrations, ideal for sharing with your emergent reader

BEGINNING READING
Short sentences, familiar words, and simple concepts for children eager to read on their own

READING WITH HELP
Engaging stories, longer sentences, and language play for developing readers

READING ALONE
Complex plots, challenging vocabulary, and high-interest topics for the independent reader

ADVANCED READING
Short paragraphs, chapters, and exciting themes for the perfect bridge to chapter books

I Can Read Books have introduced children to the joy of reading since 1957. Featuring award-winning authors and illustrators and a fabulous cast of beloved characters, I Can Read Books set the standard for beginning readers.

A lifetime of discovery begins with the magical words "I Can Read!"

Visit www.icanread.com for information
on enriching your child's reading experience.

Marley Learns a Lesson Copyright © 2013 by John Grogan All rights reserved. Manufactured in China. No part of this book may be used or reproduced in any manner whatsoever without written permission except in the case of brief quotations embodied in critical articles and reviews. For information address HarperCollins Children's Books, a division of HarperCollins Publishers, 10 East 53rd Street, New York, NY 10022.
www.icanread.com

Library of Congress catalog card number: 2012942502
ISBN 978-0-06-207487-4 (trade bdg.)—ISBN 978-0-06-207486-7 (pbk.)

12 13 14 15 16 SCP 10 9 8 7 6 5 4 3 2 1   ❖   First Edition

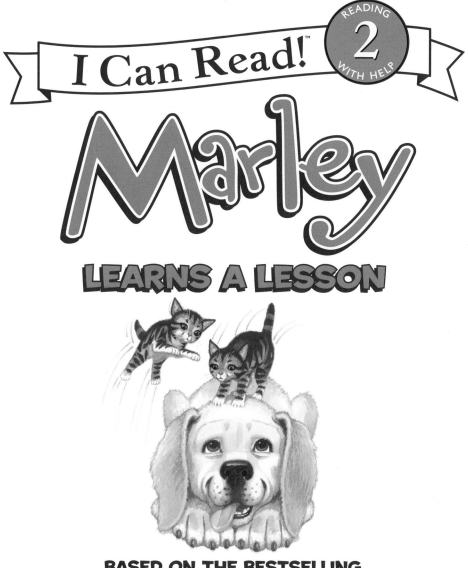

I Can Read!

READING 2 WITH HELP

Marley

LEARNS A LESSON

BASED ON THE BESTSELLING BOOKS BY JOHN GROGAN

COVER ART BY RICHARD COWDREY

TEXT BY CAITLIN BIRCH

INTERIOR ILLUSTRATIONS BY RICK WHIPPLE

HARPER

An Imprint of HarperCollinsPublishers

Cassie's family had two new kittens.

Their names were Lucky and Yow-Yow.

Marley loved Lucky and Yow-Yow.

He wanted to teach them

all of life's important things.

Marley showed Lucky and Yow-Yow
that the kittens in the mirror
are not real kittens.

Marley taught the kittens to wait

by the door for Cassie

to come home from school.

Marley taught the kittens

not to get too close

to Baby Louie's diaper.

"Danger!" warned Marley.

Lucky and Yow-Yow wanted

to teach Marley

some new things, too.

The kittens taught Marley

how to pounce.

The kittens taught Marley
their favorite game.

The kittens taught Marley

how to sharpen his claws.

"No, Marley, no!" Mommy yelled.

"Go to your doghouse, Marley.

We are going out for a little bit."

But Mommy didn't say that Marley

had to go to the doghouse

all by himself.

Marley led Lucky and Yow-Yow out

to his doghouse.

At first it was fun outside,

but then Marley heard a low rumble.

A storm was coming.

Marley did not like storms.

Soon, thunder rolled.

Lightning flashed.

Marley was scared.

Marley ran back inside.

Howwwwwwl!

Marley showed the kittens
how to howl at something scary.

The kittens didn't howl.

The kittens didn't cry.

They curled up with Marley.

Marley felt their soft fur.

He heard their gentle purring.

Boooom went the thunder.

Crack went the lightning.

And then, as quickly as it
had come,
the storm was gone.
All was well again.

Marley felt better.

"Maybe storms aren't so scary
after all," Marley thought.
He felt so much better
that he fell asleep.

When Marley woke up,
the family was home.
"Marley and the kittens
weathered the storm just fine,"
Daddy said.

Yow-Yow yawned and stretched.

Lucky licked Marley's paw.

Marley felt so happy,

he wished he could learn

how to purr.

Cataloging-in-Publication Data has been applied for and may be obtained from the Library of Congress.

Hardcover ISBN: 978-1-4197-1380-4
Paperback ISBN: 978-1-4197-1597-6

Printed and bound in China
10 9 8 7 6 5 4 3 2 1

Amulet Books are available at special discounts when purchased in quantity for premiums and promotions as well as fundraising or educational use. For details, contact specialmarkets@abramsbooks.com, or the address below.

ABRAMS
THE ART OF BOOKS SINCE 1949
115 West 18th Street
New York, NY 10011
www.abramsbooks.com

ERIC COLOSSAL

AMULET BOOKS
NEW YORK

Lay him down here.

LET'S GET COOKING!

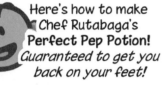

Here's how to make Chef Rutabaga's **Perfect Pep Potion!** *Guaranteed to get you back on your feet!*

Slice Honey Spice Root into fours and place in Juicer.

Ingredients

One White-Tipped Honey Spice Root

Corkscrew Juicer

Sweetened Blood Berries

Parasol Stem

JUICE IT!   Add Blood Berries to taste.   **SHAKE IT!**

Add Parasol Stem for a garnish and serve!

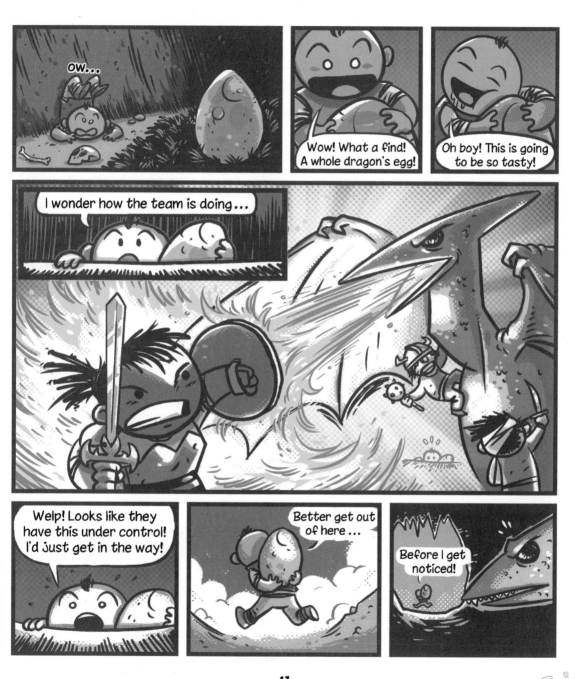

23

28

END OF
CHAPTER ONE

41

45

sigh...

Well, I can try making some soup, I GUESS!

Let's get cooking

1. One puck of dehydrated portable chicken stock.

2. Your favorite herbs and seasonings and PLENTY of butter!

3. A nice 2-pound King's Head Squash, cleaned and cut.

4. Prepare the stock as normal and add all ingredients.

5. When the squash is tender, puree it through a drum sieve.

KING'S HEAD SQUASH SOUP

53

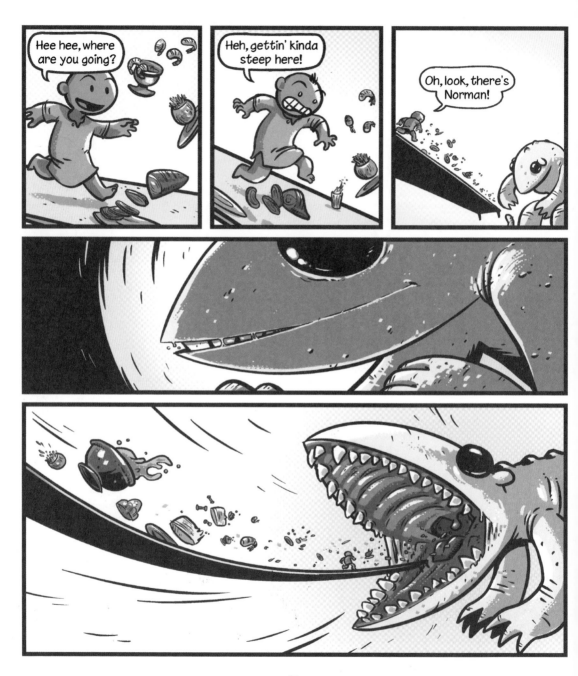

END OF
CHAPTER TWO

The ditch was searched and searched, but no one could find his head.

But That Autumn...

A new type of plant, the likes of which no one had seen before, grew out of the ditch!

It was delicious too!

King's Head Squash Soup and Crackers

King's Head Squash Pie

King's Head Squash Bread with Pineapple Slices

King's Head Squash Facial Scrub for Smoother Skin!

The castle was converted into a HUGE bakery centered around their strange new and delicious crop.

73

74

Cookin' with Cookie!

1. Get yerself a pot.

2. A big ol' scoop from that barrel over there.

3. Add water and boil it until it's edible.

4. Scoop out a handful and serve hot.

You've made...

FOOD
(WITH SCRAPINGS)

Eat it and shut up!

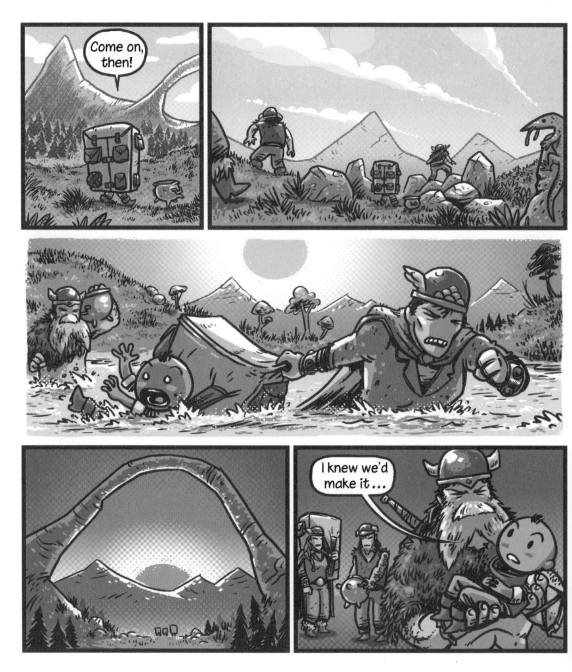

94

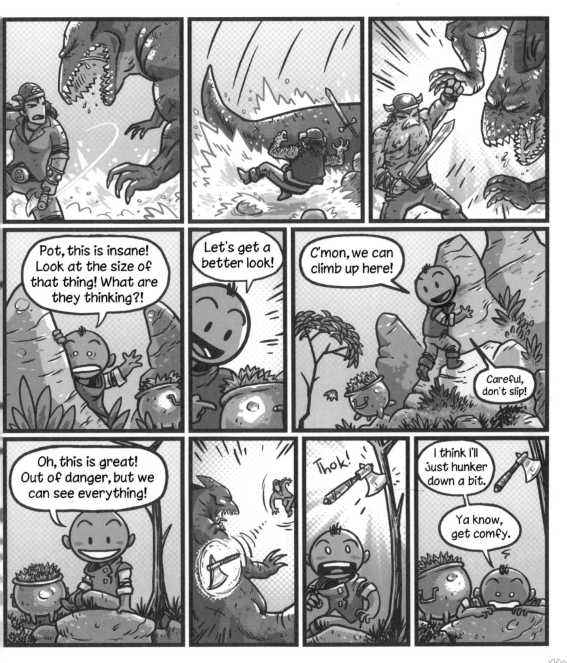

110

What happened?

We had all gathered in the Great Hall for a feast.

The doors flew open, and a frightened farmer came running in.

It was our mother's birthday.

Through gasping breaths, the farmer told us that a Koraknis had broken into the stables and was killing the livestock. Our queen was first out the door to confront it... As we raced after her, we could hear the sounds of battle ahead of us. By the time we got there...

There were nothing but footprints and blood on the ground.

113

Thank you, Thyr, for carrying Pot! Thank you, Gyda, for the fire!

And thank you, Oleg, for preparing the meat! Now, without further ado!

Let's Get Cooking!

1. First off, Koraknis meat is TOUGH! Get out your meat mallet ...

2. And just go to town on it!

WACK WACK WACK

3. In a bowl toss some spinach, brined cheese, and fresh garlic.

4. Spread mixture on flattened steaks.

5. Roll 'em up! Secure 'em with a skewer!

6. Cook for 5 minutes on each side.

You've made

STUFFED KORAKNIS SPINWHEELS!

WITH
SLICED PYKA'S PALM

117

121

END OF
CHAPTER FOUR

CHOCOLATE-DIPPED DRAGON CLAWS

INGREDIENTS

- 2 ripe bananas
- 6 ounces melting chocolate, any color (I like to use red!)
- 2 tablespoons vegetable oil
- a box of wooden Popsicle sticks

Peel the bananas and cut them in half.

Gently press a wooden Popsicle stick into the flat end of the banana.

CHOP!

Place them on a baking sheet lined with parchment paper and freeze for 15 to 30 minutes.

Melt chocolate together with vegetable oil according to package instructions.

Dip!

STOP! GET AN ADULT'S HELP WHEN HEATING ANYTHING ON THE STOVE OR IN THE MICROWAVE!

Chocolate should be very smooth.

Transfer chocolate to a tall glass for easy dipping.

Take the bananas out of the freezer and dip them one at a time into the chocolate so they are almost completely covered.

Allow excess chocolate to drip off back into glass.

RAR!

Place chocolate-covered bananas back on parchment after chocolate has hardened a little.

Freeze for another 15 to 30 minutes or until chocolate has hardened completely!

You have made

CHOCOLATE-DIPPED DRAGON CLAWS

CHOCOLATE PEANUT BUTTER POTS

INGREDIENTS

- 1/2 cup creamy peanut butter
- 1 cup powdered sugar
- 8 ounces melting chocolate
- raisins

Got a peanut allergy but still want to make this recipe? Go ahead and use a marshmallow instead of peanut butter!

-R

Dump peanut butter into a large bowl and gradually mix in powdered sugar.

This isn't really an exact science, so just keep adding sugar until the peanut butter has lost its stickiness and turned into a big doughy ball.

Refrigerate dough ball for about 10 to 15 minutes.

Tear bits off with your fingers, roll them into balls about an inch wide, and place them on a baking sheet lined with parchment paper.

After you've run out of dough, refrigerate the balls for another 20 minutes.

STOP! Melt chocolate according to package instructions.

GET AN ADULT'S HELP WHEN HEATING ANYTHING ON THE STOVE OR IN THE MICROWAVE!

Use a toothpick to pick up and dip the peanut butter balls (one at a time) into the chocolate. Allow excess to drip off.

Place back on baking sheet and press 4 raisins into the top of the chocolate.

Refrigerate one more time for 20 minutes!

When finished, pop them off the parchment paper and stand them up on the raisin feet!

You have made

CHOCOLATE PEANUT BUTTER POTS!

SO CUTE!

SO Delicious!

RUTABAGA'S PERFECT PEP POTION!

INGREDIENTS

- cranberry juice
- apple juice
- cinnamon breath mints

Yum!

Place 15 cinnamon breath mints in a plastic bag and seal it tight! Then wrap the bag in a dish towel.

Take a rolling pin or hammer and smash them to dust!

STOP! GET AN ADULT'S PERMISSION BEFORE SMASHING ANYTHING ON THEIR NICE COUNTERTOP!

Pour 1/2 cup of cranberry juice and 1/2 cup of apple juice into a large glass.

Stir in the smashed candy dust.

Fill the glass full of ice and drink up!

WHAK

You have made

PERFECT PEP POTION!

If it's too spicy, try using fewer cinnamon mints! If it's not spicy enough, add as many as you can handle!

Be wary of dragon breath!

Fwoooosh!

ERIC COLOSSAL is an artist living and working in Upstate New York. His great loves are his cats, Juju and Bear; his lovely girlfriend, Jess; and eating. He is currently working on a magic spell that lets him eat all he wants, without the unhealthy side effects. It's a work in progress.